To my wife, who taught me how to cook — V.D.P.

To the memory of my mom, who introduced me to Brer Rabbit in 1946 — B.M.

Brer Rabbit and His Family

Jump
On Over!

The Adventures of Brer Rabbit
and His Family

BY JOEL CHANDLER HARRIS

ADAPTED BY VAN DYKE PARKS   ILLUSTRATED BY BARRY MOSER

VOYAGER BOOKS
HARCOURT BRACE & COMPANY
San Diego   New York   London

Library of Congress Cataloging-in-Publication Data
Parks, Van Dyke.
Jump on over!: the adventures of Brer Rabbit and his family/by
Joel Chandler Harris; adapted by Van Dyke Parks; illustrated by
Barry Moser.—1st ed.
p. cm.
"Voyager Books."
Summary: A collection of five tales in which Brer Rabbit outwits Brer Fox,
Brer Wolf, and Brer Bear in order to ensure his family's survival during a drought.
ISBN 0-15-241354-5
ISBN 0-15-201707-0 pb
1. Afro-Americans—Folklore. 2. Tales—Southern states. [1. Folklore,
Afro-American. 2. Animals—Folklore.] I. Harris, Joel Chandler, 1848–1908.
II. Moser, Barry, ill. III. Title.
PZ8.1.P2236Ju   1989
[398.2]—dc19   89-7417

F E D C B A

Printed in Singapore

The illustrations in this book, both black-and-white and color, were executed with transparent
watercolor on paper handmade for the Royal Watercolor Society in 1982 by J. Barcham Greene.
The calligraphy was done by Reassurance Wunder, West Hatfield, Massachusetts.
Text and display types in Cochin by Thompson Type, San Diego, California
Color separations by Heinz Weber, Inc., Los Angeles, California
Printed and bound by Tien Wah Press, Singapore
Production supervision by Stanley Redfern and Jane Van Gelder
Designed by Barry Moser

Contents

ILLUSTRATOR'S NOTE   vii

Stories and *Pictures*

Brer Rabbit and His Family   ii

How Brer Rabbit Frightened His Neighbors   3
Brer Rabbit Puttin' In His Goober Patch   2
Waitin' for the Day   4
Ol' Man Spewter-Splutter   6
Brer Bear & the Stump   8

Brer Rabbit and Brer Bear   11
Brer Fox Puttin' In His Goober Patch   10
Brer Fox Settin' His Trap   12
Brer Rabbit, Hangin' in the Elements   14
Brer Bear, Makin' a Dollar a Minute   15
Brer Rabbit in the Mudhole   16

Why Brer Wolf Didn't Eat the Little Rabs   19
Brer Wolf & Brer Fox, Waitin'   18
Headin' Off down the Road   20
Nothin' but a Jug of Molasses   22
All Safe & Sound   24

Another Story about the Little Rabs   27
Brer Fox Drops By   26
The Little Bird a-Singin'   28

Brer Fox Gets Out-Foxed   31
Brer Rabbit & Brer Fox Survey the Drought   30
The Wagon & Team   32
One from Six   34
Brer Fox Fetches One Big Pull   36-37
Out Cold   38

Song: "Home"   40

Illustrator's Note

I first came to know the adventures of Brer Rabbit in 1946. They were my favorite stories, and I grew to love them even more when I had children of my own and read these tales to them. Consequently, when I began designing and illustrating books, the Brer Rabbit stories were among the literary works that interested me most.

The origin of these folktales is complex and difficult to trace. For more than a hundred years they were told and retold by slaves in the American South — long before Georgian newspaperman Joel Chandler Harris collected them in the late nineteenth century. Harris invented a black slave character named Uncle Remus, who told the Brer Rabbit stories to a young white boy. He published his first volume, *Uncle Remus: His Songs and His Sayings*, in 1880. Coincidentally, one of the two illustrators of that collection was James H. Moser[1] — although most people believe the first edition to be the one that followed, which was illustrated by A. B. Frost.

The images in my watercolors are collected from various sources: my imagination, the extraordinary work of A. B. Frost, and nineteenth-[2] and twentieth-[3]century photographs. The task of an illustrator is to add dimension to a text and offer suggestions to the reader. The illustrator can even bring the nineteenth century into the twentieth century without jarring the reader — by subtle use of anachronism in costume and setting. Examples are the Burma Shave sign in *Jump!*, the Coca-Cola sign in *Jump Again!*, and the bibbed overalls in *Jump On Over!*

I have tried to invent images true to the spirit of the stories and the characters: Brer Bear is a little slow, Brer Fox and Brer Wolf are eager to dine upon the little Rabs, and Brer Rabbit always has a twinkle in his eye.

Harris has been both applauded and deeply criticized for his portrayal of the Old South, yet the animal tales themselves are timeless. Overall, what has been most important to me is the underlying moral that brute strength is no match for cleverness, quickness, and the power of humor in times of hardship. Wherever you are, you can find a laughing place and your own briarpatch.

— *B.M.*

[1]The other illustrator was Frederick S. Church.
[2]By Timothy H. O'Sullivan, Matthew Brady, among others.
[3]By Doris Ulmann, Eudora Welty, Walker Evans, among others.

Jump
On Over!

The Adventures of Brer Rabbit
and His Family

Bier Rabbit Puttin' In His Goober Patch

*W*AY back yonder, before your mama and daddy were born, before any of us were born, animals had lots more sense than they do now. They sauntered around the same as folks do today, but none of them was brash enough to catch up with Brer Rabbit.

Under his hat, when he wore one, Brer Rabbit had a mighty quick thinking apparatus, and the pranks he played on other folks pestered them both ways — a-coming and a-going. Brer Fox and Brer Wolf and Brer Bear were always laying traps for him and getting caught in them themselves, and day in and day out they were making plans to cook Brer Rabbit and his family in their dinner pots.

All this scrabbling to stay alive was hard enough, but Tribulation, seemed like she was always waiting around the corner. There came a time of famine, and victuals were monstrous scarce and money mighty slack. As long as there were any victuals going around, Brer Rabbit was bound to get his family their share, but by and by, it came to pass that Brer Rabbit's stomach began to pinch him.

He put two and two together, and the notion struck him that he'd better be home looking after the interests of his family instead of traipsing and trolloping around to all the frolics in the settlement. He took and studied this in his mind, until by and by, he set out to determine his own livelihood.

So Brer Rabbit up and planted himself a fine crop of goober peas. He allowed, he did, that if they fetched him anywhere near the money he expected they would, he'd go to town and buy what necessity had called for.

No sooner had he said that than his wife, Miss Molly, she vowed, she

Waitin' for the Day

did, that it was a scandal and a shame if he didn't whirl in and get seven tin cups for the children to drink out of, and seven tin platters for them to sop up their supper out of, and a coffeepot for the family. Brer Rabbit, he allowed that was exactly what he was going to do, and he said, he did, that he was going to town that coming Wednesday.

Brer Rabbit set out for his goober patch, and he wasn't more than out of the gate before Miss Molly slapped on her bonnet, she did, and rushed across to her friend Miss Mink's house. She hadn't been there a minute before she up and told Miss Mink that Brer Rabbit had promised to go to town that coming Wednesday to get the children something.

When Mr. Mink came home, Miss Mink up and allowed she wanted to know why he couldn't buy something for *his* children, the same as Brer Rabbit was doing, and they quarreled and they quarreled, just like folks do now.

Miss Mink, she carried the news to Miss Fox, and then Brer Fox, he got a raking over the coals. Miss Fox told Miss Wolf, and Miss Wolf told Miss Bear, and it wasn't long before everybody in Hominy Grove knew that Brer Rabbit was going to town that coming Wednesday to get his children something. And all the other folks' children asked their mamas why their daddys couldn't get them something. So there it went.

After that, Brer Fox and Brer Wolf and Brer Bear, they made up their minds, they did, that if they ever had a reason to catch up with Brer Rabbit, this was the time, and they fixed up a plan. They'd lay in the bushes for Brer Rabbit and nab him when he came back from town. They made all their arrangements and waited for the day.

Sure enough, when Wednesday came, Brer Rabbit ate his breakfast before sunup, and he put out for town terbuckity-buckity. He got himself a plug of Rabbit tobacco and a pocket handkerchief, and he got Miss Molly a coffeepot, and he got the children seven tin cups and seven tin platters, and then, toward sundown, he started back home.

He lippity-clipped along, he did, feeling mighty biggity, but by and by, when he got sort of tired, he sat down under a blackjack tree and began to fan himself with one of the platters.

While he was doing this, a little bitty teensy sapsucker ran up and down the tree and kept on making a mighty queer racket. After a while, Brer

Ol' Man Spewter-Splutter

Rabbit shoo'd at him with the platter. This made the teensy little sapsucker mighty mad, and he rushed out on a limb right over Brer Rabbit, and he sang out:

Twiddly-dee, twiddly-dee!
I can see what you don't see!
Twiddly-dee, twiddly-dee!
I can see what you don't see!

He kept on singing this, he did, until Brer Rabbit began to look around, and no sooner did he do this than he saw marks in the sand where someone had been there before him. He looked a little closer, and then he saw what the sapsucker was driving at. He scratched his head, Brer Rabbit did, and he allowed to himself:

"Heyo! Here's where Brer Fox has been sitting, and there's the print of his nice bushy tail. Here's where Brer Wolf's been sitting, and there's the print of his fine long tail. Here's where Brer Bear's been squatting on his haunches, and there's the print where he hasn't got a tail. They've all been here, and I lay they're hiding out in the big gully down there in the hollow."

With that, ol' man Rab put his belongings in the bushes, and then he ran 'way around to see what he could see. Sure enough, when Brer Rabbit got over to the big gully down in the hollow, there they were. Brer Fox, he was on one side of the road, and Brer Wolf was on the other side, and ol' Brer Bear, he was curled up in the gully taking a nap.

Brer Rabbit took a peep at them, he did, and he licked his foot and slicked back his hair, and then he held his hands across his mouth and laughed.

He grinned, he did, and then he lit out to where he left his belongings, and when he got there, he danced around and slapped himself on the leg and made all sorts of curious motions. Then he got to work and turned the coffeepot upside down and stuck it on his head; then he ran his suspenders through the handles of the cups; then he divided the platters, some in one hand and some in the other. After he was good and ready, he crept to the top of the hill, he did, and took a running start and flew down like a hurricane — *rickety, rackety, slambang!*

Brer Bear & the Stump

Bless your soul, these folks never heard a fuss like that, and they never saw a man that looked like Brer Rabbit did, with the coffeepot on his head, the tin cups a-rattling on his shoulders, and the platters a-waving and a-shining in the air.

Now, mind you, ol' Brer Bear was lying in the gully taking a nap, and the fuss scared him so bad that he made a break and ran over Brer Fox. He rushed out in the road, he did, and when he saw the sight, he whirled around and ran back over Brer Wolf. With the scrambling and the scuffling, Brer Rabbit got right on them before they could get away. He hollered out, he did:

"Give me room! Turn me loose! I'm ol' man Spewter-Splutter with long claws, and scales on my back! I'm snaggletoothed and double-jointed! Give me room!"

Every time he'd fetch a whoop, he'd rattle the cups and slap the platters together — *rickety, rackety, slambang!* And when those folks got their limbs together, they split the wind, they did.

Ol' Brer Bear, he crashed into a stump standing in his way, and there's no point in telling how he pulled it up because nobody would believe it. But the next morning, Brer Rabbit and his children went back there, they did, and they got enough splinters to make kindling wood for the whole winter. And you best believe that when Miss Molly's friends came visiting, they made a great fuss of admiration over those platters, cups, and coffeepot, and there wasn't a moment's peace when they got home.

A long time after that, Brer Rabbit came upon Brer Fox and Brer Wolf and Brer Bear, and he got behind the briars, Brer Rabbit did, and he hollered out, "I'm ol' man Spewter-Splutter with long claws, and scales on my back! I'm snaggletoothed and double-jointed, and you're the ones I'm after!"

Brer Fox and Brer Wolf and Brer Bear, they took to their heels and made a break for the woods. But before they got out of sight and out of hearing, Brer Rabbit jumped out and showed himself, he did. Then he lay down in that briar patch and rolled and laughed till his sides hurt, and he laughed once more for good measure. It surely was scandalous the way Brer Rabbit could laugh. Brer Fox was after him, Brer Wolf was after him, and Brer Bear was after him, but they hadn't caught him yet.

Brer Fox Puttin' In His Gooter Patch

*T*HAT same year it fell out that the crops burnt up. A dry spell had done the work, and if you'd have struck a match anywhere, the whole county would have blazed up. Old Man Hungriness just naturally took off his clothes and went parading about everywhere, and folks got bony and skinny.

In those days, most everybody lived in the same settlement. They had their fusses, but they didn't have any lasting falling out, and they lived just as satisfactual as folks do now. But times got mighty hard, and it was about all they could do just to make ends meet. Rake and scrape as they could, some of them would have to go hungry.

So Brer Fox said to himself that he expected he'd better plant a goober patch of his own, and in those days, it was touch and go. The word wasn't more than out of his mouth before the ground was broken up and the goobers were planted. He watered it with every drop he could find, and then he watered it some more.

Ol' Brer Rabbit, his patch was long gone. He sat off and watched the motions, he did, and he sort of shut one eye and sang to his hungry little Rabs:

> *Sittin' by the roadside on a summer's day*
> *Chattin' with my young 'uns, passin' time away*
> *Layin' in the shadow underneath the trees*
> *Goodness how delicious! Eating goober peas . . .*

Brer Fox Settin' His Trap

Sure enough, when the goobers began to ripen up, every time Brer Fox went down to his patch, he found that somebody'd been grabbing amongst the vines, and he got mighty mad. He sort of suspected who that somebody was, but Brer Rabbit, he covered his tracks so cute that Brer Fox didn't know how to catch him.

By and by, one day Brer Fox took a walk all around his pea patch, and it wasn't long before he found a crack in the fence where the rail had been rubbed smooth, and right there he set up a trap. He bent down a hickory sapling, growing in the fence corner, and he tied one end to a plowline on the top, and on the other end he fixed a loop knot, and he fastened that with a trigger right in the crack.

The next morning, when Brer Rabbit slipped up and crept through the crack, the loop knot caught him behind the forelegs, and the sapling flew up, and there he was, hanging betwixt heaven and earth. Back and forth he swung. He feared he was going to fall, and he feared he wasn't going to fall.

While he was a-fixing up a tale for Brer Fox, he heard a lumbering down the road, and presently along came Ol' Brer Bear, ambling back from where he'd been taking a beehive.

Brer Rabbit hailed him, "Howdy, Brer Bear!"

Brer Bear, he looked around, and by and by, he saw Brer Rabbit swinging from the sapling, and he hollered out, "Heyo, Brer Rabbit! How you come on this morning?"

"Much obliged, I'm fair to middling, Brer Bear," said Brer Rabbit, said he.

Then Brer Bear, he asked Brer Rabbit what he was doing, hanging up there in the elements, and Brer Rabbit, he up and said he was making a dollar a minute. Brer Bear, he wanted to know how. Brer Rabbit, he said he was keeping crows out of Brer Fox's pea patch, and then he asked Brer Bear if he didn't want to make a dollar a minute.

Brer Bear had a big family of children to take care of, and he'd make such a nice scarecrow.

Brer Bear allowed that he'd take the job, and then Brer Rabbit showed him how to bend down the sapling, and it wasn't long before Brer Bear was caught in Brer Rabbit's place. Then Brer Rabbit, he put out for Brer Fox's house, and when he got there, he sang out, "Brer Fox! Oh, Brer Fox! Come

Brer Rabbit, Hangin' in the Elements

Brer Bear, Makin' a Dollar a Minute

Brer Rabbit in the Mudhole

out here, Brer Fox, and I'll show you the one who's been stealing your goober peas."

Brer Fox, he grabbed up his walking stick, and both of them went running back down to the goober patch. When they got there, sure enough, there was Ol' Brer Bear.

"Oh, yes, you're caught now," said Brer Fox. And before Brer Bear could explain, Brer Rabbit jumped up and down, and he hollered out, "Hit him in the mouth, Brer Fox," and Brer Fox, he drew back with his walking cane, and he *blippity-blipped* him, and every time Brer Bear tried to explain, Brer Fox showered down on him with his cane.

While all this was going on, Brer Rabbit, he slipped off and got in a mudhole and left just his eyes sticking out, because he knew that Brer Bear would be coming along after him. Sure enough, by and by, there came Brer Bear down the road, and when he got to the mudhole, he said, "Howdy, Brer Frog. Have you seen Brer Rabbit go by?"

"He just went by," said Brer Rabbit, said he, and ol' Brer Bear took off down the road like a mule.

Brer Rabbit, he came out and dried himself in the sun, and he capered around there for some time. Then he put out for home, and, like he most always did, he went home a-laughing. He was mighty pleased with himself. He took his children on his knee and told them a monstrous good tale about how he'd outsmarted Brer Fox and Brer Bear.

Soon word got out, and all the folks said that Brer Rabbit surely had things wrapped up around there. And that just about suited Brer Rabbit to a gnat's heel.

Brer Wolf & Brer Fox, Waitin'

*B*RER Fox and Brer Wolf lived with their families on one side of the road, and Brer Rabbit lived with his family on the other side, not close enough to quarrel about the fence line yet close enough for the youngest children to play together while folks were paying their Sunday calls.

Well, Brer Wolf wanted to eat the little Rabs all the time, but there was one time in particular they made his mouth water, and that was during a peaceful spell when he and Brer Fox were visiting at Brer Rabbit's house.

Times were hard, but the little Rabs were slick and fat and just as frisky as kittens. Brer Rabbit and his wife were off somewhere in their Sunday-go-to-meeting clothes, and Brer Wolf and Brer Fox were a-setting in front of the house waiting for them.

Sundays were mighty special; they were mighty friendly. Brer Fox was chewing his tobacco and spitting in the dust. Brer Wolf, he was grinning about old times and picking his teeth, which looked mighty white and sharp. They were setting there, they were, just as thick as fleas on a dog's back, looking like butter wouldn't melt in their mouths.

Headin' off Down the Road

The little Rabs were playing around, and though they were little, they kept their ears open. Brer Wolf looked at them out of the corner of his eye, and he licked his chops and winked at Brer Fox, and Brer Fox winked back at him. Brer Wolf crossed his legs, and Brer Fox crossed his, too. The little Rabs, they frisked and they frolicked.

Brer Wolf allowed, "They're mighty fat."

Brer Fox grinned and said, "Man, hush your mouth. It's Sunday!"

Brer Wolf looked at them and allowed, "Aren't they slick and pretty?"

Brer Fox chuckled and said, "Oh, I wish you'd hush!"

The little Rabs played farther and farther off, but they kept their eyes open.

Brer Wolf smacked his mouth and allowed, "They're juicy and tender."

Brer Fox followed his eyes and said, "Man, can't you hush up before you give me the fidgets?"

The little Rabs, they frisked and they frolicked, but they kept their ears wide open.

Then Brer Wolf made a bargain with Brer Fox that when Brer Rabbit and his missus got home, one would get Brer Rabbit wrapped up in a dispute about first something and then another, while the other one would go out and catch Miss Molly and the little Rabs.

Brer Fox allowed, "You'd better do the talking, Brer Wolf, and let me coax the little Rabs off. I've got more winning ways with womenfolk and children than you do."

Brer Wolf said, "You can't made a gourd out of a pumpkin, Brer Fox. I ain't no talker. Your tongue is lots slicker than mine. I can bite lots better than I can talk. Those little Rabs and the missus don't need coaxing; they need catching — that's what they need. You keep ol' Brer Rabbit busy, and I'll tend to the little Rabs.

Both of them knew that whoever caught the little Rabs, the other one wasn't going to smell hide nor hair of them, and Brer Fox and Brer Wolf flew up and got to disputing, and while they were disputing and going on that way, the little Rabs put off down the road blickety-blickety — to meet their mama and daddy. Because they knew that if they stayed there, they'd get in big trouble.

They went off down the road, the little Rabs did, and they hadn't gone

Nothin' But a Jug of Molasses

far before they met their daddy and their mama coming along home. Brer Rabbit had his walking cane in one hand and a jug in the other, and he looked as big as life and twice as natural.

The little Rabs ran toward them and hollered, "What you got, Daddy? What you got, Daddy?"

Brer Rabbit, he said, "Nothing but a jug of molasses."

The little Rabs hollered, "Let me taste, Daddy! Let me taste, Daddy!"

Then Brer Rabbit set the jug down in the road, and Miss Rabbit let them lick the stopper a time or two, and after they got their wind back, they up and told their papa and mama about the agreement that Brer Wolf and Brer Fox had made and about the dispute they were having.

Brer Rabbit sort of laughed to himself, and then he picked up his jug and jogged on toward home. When he was almost there, he stopped and told Miss Rabbit and the little Rabs to stay back there out of sight, to wait until he called them.

The little Rabs and their mama, they were mighty glad to do this, because they knew about Brer Wolf's big toofies and Brer Fox's red tongue, and they huddled up as still as a mouse in the flour barrel.

Brer Rabbit went on home alone, and, sure enough, he found Brer Wolf and Brer Fox waiting for him. They'd settled their dispute, and they were sitting there looking just as happy as a pair of bee martins with a bucket of bugs.

They passed the time of day with Brer Rabbit, and then they asked him what he had in the jug. Brer Rabbit hemmed and hawed and looked sort of solemn.

Brer Wolf looked like he was stuck on finding out what was in the jug, and he kept a-pestering Brer Rabbit about it. But Brer Rabbit just shook his head and looked solemn and talked about the weather and the crops, and one thing and another.

By and by, Brer Fox made out that he was going after a drink of water, and he slipped out, he did, to catch Miss Molly and the little Rabs. And as soon as he got out of the house, Brer Rabbit looked all around to see if he was listening, and then he went to the jug and pulled out the stopper.

He handed it to Brer Wolf and said, "Taste that."

Brer Wolf tasted the molasses, and he smacked his mouth.

All Safe & Sound

He allowed, "What kind of sweetness is that? It sure is good."

Brer Rabbit got up close to Brer Wolf and said, "Don't tell nobody. It's Fox blood."

Brer Wolf looked astonished. He allowed, "How do you know?"

Brer Rabbit said, "I know what I know!"

Brer Wolf said, "Give me some more!"

Brer Rabbit said, "You can get some more for yourself easy enough, and the fresher it is, the better."

Brer Wolf allowed, "How do you know?"

Brer Rabbit said, "I know what I know!"

With that, Brer Wolf stepped out and started toward Brer Fox.

Brer Fox saw him coming, and he sort of backed off. Brer Wolf got a little closer, and by and by, he made a dash at Brer Fox.

Brer Fox dodged, he did, and then he put out for the woods with Brer Wolf right at his heels. Brer Fox had learned his lesson, at least for now.

Then, after so long a time, after Brer Rabbit got done laughing, he called to his family, and he and Miss Rabbit gave the little Rabs some molasses, and then they sent them to bed.

Brer Fox Drops By

Another Story about the Little Rabs

FIND 'em where you will and when you may; good children always get taken care of. Brer Rabbit's children, they minded their daddy and mama from day's end to day's end. When ol' man Rabbit said "Scoot," they scooted, and when Miss Rabbit said "Scat," they scatted. They did that. And they kept their clothes clean, and they had no smut under their noses.

They were good children, and if they hadn't been, there was one time when there wouldn't have been any little Rabs — not a one.

There came a time when Brer Fox dropped in at Brer Rabbit's house again and didn't find anybody there except the little Rabs. Brer Rabbit, he was off somewhere raiding on a collard patch, and Miss Rabbit, she was attending a quilting in the neighborhood, and while the little Rabs were playing hide-and-seek — *switch*, in dropped Brer Fox.

The little Rabs were so fat they fairly made his mouth water, but he remembered how Brer Rabbit tricked Brer Wolf into thinking molasses was Fox blood, and he was scared to gobble them up right then and there without a good excuse. The little Rabs, they were mighty skittish, and they sort of huddled themselves together and watched Brer Fox's motions. Brer Fox, he sat there and studied what sort of excuse he was going to make up.

By and by, he saw a great big stalk of sugarcane standing up in the corner, and he cleared up his throat and talked biggity:

"You! You young Rabs there, sail around here and break me a piece of that sweetening tree," said he, and then he coughed.

The little Rabs, they got out the sugarcane, they did, and they wrastled with it and sweated over it, but it wasn't any use. They couldn't break it. Brer Fox, he made like he wasn't watching, but he kept on hollering:

"Hurry up there, Rabs! I'm waitin' on you."

And the little Rabs, they hustled 'round and wrastled with it, but they couldn't break it. By and by, they heard a little bird singing on top of the house, and the song that the little bird sang was this here:

Use your toothies to gnaw it,
Use your toothies to saw it,
Saw it and take it,
And then you can break it.

Then the little Rabs, they got mighty glad, and they gnawed the cane almost before Brer Fox could get his legs uncrossed, and when they carried him the sugarcane, Brer Fox, he sat there and studied how he was going to make up some other excuse for nabbing them. By and by, he stood up and got down the sifter that was hanging on the wall, and he hollered out:

"Come here, Rabs! Take this here sifter and run down to the spring and fetch me some fresh water."

The little Rabs, they ran down to the spring and tried to dip up the water with the sifter, but of course it all ran out, and it kept on running out, until by and by, the little Rabs sat down and began to cry. Then the little bird sitting up in the tree, he began to sing, and this is the song he sang:

Sifter holds water same as a tray
If you fill it with moss and dab it with clay;
The Fox gets madder the longer you stay —
Fill it with moss and dab it with clay.

Up they jumped, the little Rabs did, and they fixed the sifter so it wouldn't leak, and then they carried the water to old Brer Fox. Then Brer Fox, he got mighty mad, and pointed at a big stick of wood and told the little Rabs to put that on the fire. The little Rabs, they got around the wood, they did, and they lifted it so hard they could see their own sins, but the wood, it didn't budge. Then they heard the little bird singing, and this is the song he sang:

Spit in your hands, and tug it, and roll it,
And get behind it, and push it, and pull it;
Spit in your hands, and rear back, and roll it.

And just about the time they got the wood on the fire, their daddy, he came skipping in, and the little bird, he flew away. Brer Fox, he saw his game was up, and it wasn't long before he made his excuse and started to go.

"You'd better stay and take a snack with me, Brer Fox," said Brer Rabbit, said he. "Since Brer Wolf quit coming and sharing my molasses with me, I'm getting so I feel right lonesome these long nights," said he.

But Brer Fox, he buttoned up his coat collar tight and just put out for home.

Brer Rabbit & Brer Fox Survey the Drought

Brer Fox Gets Out-Foxed

*T*HE same year the crops burnt up, the seasons just took and came wrong. One week after another the weather got even hotter, and it seemed like every natural leaf on the trees was going to turn to powder.

The ground looked like it had been cooked. Even the goober patches were all parched up, and there were no crops anywhere. Folks didn't know what to do. They ran this a-way, and they ran that a-way; yet when they quit running, they didn't know where their bread was coming from. This was the way it looked to Brer Fox, so one day when he had a mighty hankering for something sort of scrumptious, he met Brer Rabbit in the lane, and he said to him, said he:

"Brer Rabbit, whereabouts is our bread coming from?"

Brer Rabbit, he bowed, he did, and he said, said he:

"Looks like it might be coming from nowhere," said he.

Well, he joked and he joked, but by and by, he didn't feel like any more joking, and then he up and said, said he, that he and Brer Fox better start out and take their families with them to town and swap them off for some

31

The Wagon & Team

fresh-ground cornmeal. And Brer Fox said, said he, that this looked fair and square, and then they made their agreements.

Brer Fox was to supply the wagon and team, and he promised that he was going to catch his family and tie them hard and fast with a red twine string.

Brer Rabbit, he said, said he, that he was going to catch his family and tie them all and meet Brer Fox at the fork of the road.

Sure enough, soon in the morning, when Brer Fox drew up with the wagon, he hollered, "Whoa!" and Brer Rabbit, he hollered back, "Whoa yourself!" and then Brer Fox knew they were all there. Brer Fox, he sat up on the seat, and all of his family, they were a-laying under the seat in back. Brer Rabbit, he put all his family in the back of the wagon, too, and he said, said he, that he expected he'd better sit there until his missus and the little Rabs got sort of used to their surroundings. Then Brer Fox cracked his whip, and off they went toward town.

Brer Fox, he hollered every once in a while:

"No nodding back there, Brer Rabbit!"

Brer Rabbit, he hollered back:

"Brer Fox, you miss the ruts and the rocks, and I'll miss the nodding."

But all that time, bless your soul! Brer Rabbit was sitting there untying Miss Molly and his seven little Rabs.

When he got them all untied, Brer Rabbit, he hoisted himself on the seat alongside Brer Fox, and they sat there and talked and laughed about the all-sorts of times they were going to have when they traded in their families for the cornmeal. Brer Fox said he was going to bake hoecake. Brer Rabbit said he was going to make ashcake.

Just about this time, one of Brer Rabbit's children raised himself up easy and hopped out of the wagon.

Miss Fox, she sang out:

One from seven
Don't leave eleven.

Brer Fox kicked his missus with his foot to make her keep still. By and by, another little Rab popped up and hopped out.

One From Six

Miss Fox sang out:

One from six
Leaves me less kicks.

Brer Fox, he went on talking to Brer Rabbit, and Brer Rabbit, he went on talking to Brer Fox, and it wasn't long before all of Brer Rabbit's family had popped up and dived out of the wagon, and every time one would go, Miss Fox, she'd sing out like she did for the others:

One from five
Leaves four alive;
One from four
Leaves three no more;
One from three
Leaves two to go free;
One from one
And they're all done.

Brer Fox looked around after a while, and when he saw that all of Brer Rabbit's family was gone, he leaned back and hollered, "Whoa!" And then he said, said he:

"In the name of goodness, Brer Rabbit! Where are all your folk?"

Brer Rabbit looked around, and then he made like he was crying. He just fairly boohooed, and then he said, said he:

"There now, Brer Fox! I just knew that if I put my missus and my poor little children in there with your folks, they'd get eaten up. I just knew it!"

Ol' Miss Fox, she just vowed she hadn't touched Brer Rabbit's family. But Brer Fox, he'd been wanting to taste those little Rabs all the way, and he begrudged them, so he was mighty mad with his ol' woman and his children, and he said, said he:

"You can just make the most of that, because I'm a-going to bid you good riddance this very day."

And sure enough, Brer Fox took his whole family to town and traded them off for cornmeal.

Brer Rabbit was with them, just as big as life. Then he and Brer Fox started back, they did, and when they got four or five miles out of town, it

crossed Brer Fox's mind that he'd come away and left a plug of chewing
tobacco in the store, and he said he believed he'd go back after it.

Brer Rabbit, he said that he'd stay and take care of the wagon while
Brer Fox ran back to get the tobacco. As soon as Brer Fox was out of sight,
Brer Rabbit laid the horses under the whip and drove the wagon home. He
put the horses in his own stable, and the cornmeal in the smokehouse, and
the wagon in the barn, and then he put some cornmeal in his pocket, and he
cut the horses' tails off. Then he went back up the road until he came to some
quicksand, and in that he stuck the tails and waited for Brer Fox.

36

After a while, along came Brer Fox, and then Brer Rabbit began to holler and pull at the tails. He said, said he:

"Run here, Brer Fox! Run here! You're just in time if you aren't too late. Run here, Brer Fox! Run here! The horses are sinking in quicksand!"

Brer Fox, he ran and jerked Brer Rabbit and said, said he: "Get out of the way, Brer Rabbit! You're too little! Get out of the way, and let a man catch hold."

Brer Fox took hold, and he fetched one big pull, and it was the only pull he made, because the tails came out, and he turned a back somersault.

Out Cold

He jumped up, he did, and began to grabble in the quicksand just as hard as he could.

Brer Rabbit, he'd been standing by, and he sprinkled some cornmeal into the quicksand when Brer Fox wasn't looking, and seeing his lost cornmeal in the quicksand made Brer Fox grabble worse and worse, and he grabbled so hard, and he grabbled so long, that it wasn't much later before he fell down in a dead faint, and that was the last of ol' Brer Fox that day and time.

Brer Rabbit, he laughed plum till morning, and then he laughed while he was racking on home. He loped a little ways and then set down by the road and laughed some more.

Well, some tell one tale, and some tell another. Some say that from that time forward, Brer Fox saw he was no match for Brer Rabbit, and all the folks in Hominy Grove made friends and stayed so. Some say they kept quarreling. Maybe it was a mix of both. But one thing's for sure — Brer Rabbit, he kept on a-laughing. And no doubt the little Rabs have been a-laughing, too, and outwitting those folks who've pursued them ever since.

Home

Music by Van Dyke Parks
Lyrics by Van Dyke Parks and Terry Gilkyson